Hot and cold

Story by Barbara Stavetski

Illustrations by Mark Weber

Dr. Judith Nadell, Series Editor

We have chicken.

Chicken is hot.

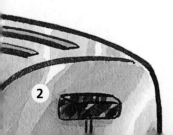

We have salad.

Salad is cold.

We have rice.

Rice is hot.

We have milk.

Milk is cold.

We have corn.

Corn is hot.

We have applesauce.

Applesauce is cold.

We have bread.

Bread is hot.

We have ice cream.

Ice cream is **very** cold.